"Quiet Please"

This story shows the value of enjoying your
own company by using your imagination.

Story by:
Phil Baron

Illustrated by:

Russell Hicks
Theresa Mazurek
Douglas McCarthy
Allyn Conley-Gorniak
Julie Ann Armstrong

Lorann Downer
Rivka
Fay Whitemountain
Suzanne Lewis
Lisa Souza

WORLDS OF WONDER™

Worlds of Wonder, Inc. is the exclusive licensee, manufacturer and distributor of the World of Teddy Ruxpin toys. "The World of Teddy Ruxpin" and "Teddy Ruxpin" are trademarks of Alchemy II, Inc., Chatsworth, CA. The symbol **W•W** and "Worlds of Wonder" are trademarks of Worlds of Wonder, Inc., Fremont, California.

ubby®   Newton Gimmick™   Princess Aruzia™   Leota™   Wooly What's-It™

Prince Arin™   Fobs®

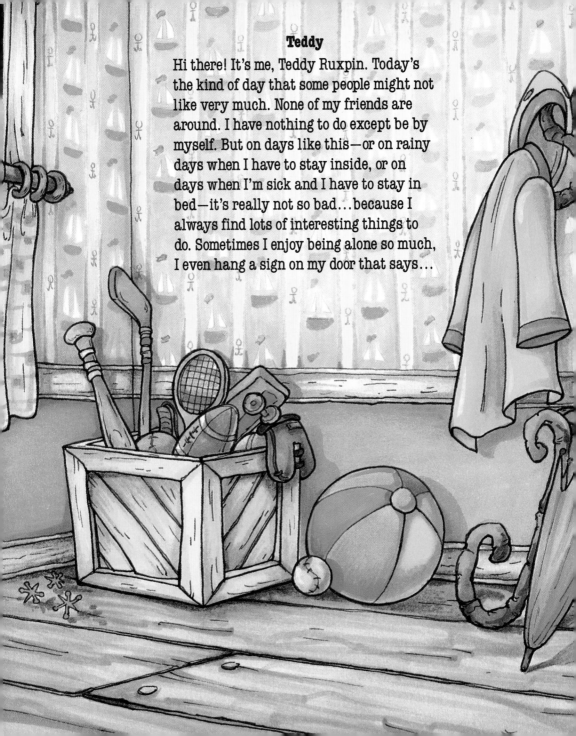

Teddy

Hi there! It's me, Teddy Ruxpin. Today's the kind of day that some people might not like very much. None of my friends are around. I have nothing to do except be by myself. But on days like this—or on rainy days when I have to stay inside, or on days when I'm sick and I have to stay in bed—it's really not so bad...because I always find lots of interesting things to do. Sometimes I enjoy being alone so much, I even hang a sign on my door that says...

Page 1

'Quiet Please''

Quiet please!
Quiet please!
It's the kind of day just made for quiet.
If I were you, I think I would try it,
And you won't need the help of anyone.
Quiet please!
Quiet please!
There is really nothing you can bring me.
I have some little songs I'd like to sing me
I'll be sitting here quietly
Having fun!

Even if the rain is pouring,
There's no need to say it's boring.
Should a little rain affect your mood.

And even if you're feeling sickly,
You'll feel better much more quickly
If you have a positively positive attitude.
You can laugh away each drizzly cloud.
So, let's quietly sing it out loud…

Quiet please!
Quiet please!
It's the kind of day just made for quiet.
If I were you, I think I would try it,
And you won't need the help of anyone.
Quiet please!
Quiet please!
There is really nothing you can buy me,
Because I have enough to occupy me.
I'll just be sitting here quietly
Having fun!

Looking out the window or imagining
   things,
Reading stories, making up your own,
Singing funny songs that no one else
   can sing,
There's a lot to do when you're alone.

Even if it's yucky weather
You'll have fun if you are clever.
There's a hundred games that you
   can play.
And even if you're feeling dizzy,
You'll feel better when you're busy
Doing the quiet stuff I always do in
   a quiet day.
By yourself is such a happy place to be,
So now quietly sing it with me!

Quiet please!
Quiet please!
It's the kind of day just made for quiet
If I were you, I think I would try it,
And you won't need the help of anyone.
Quiet please!
Quiet please!
There is really nothing you can tell me
'Cause on days like this
I might as well be
Simply sitting here quietly
Having fun!
Quiet please!

Teddy

One of the things I sang about in that song was "looking out the window." That might not sound like a very exciting thing to do, but you'd be amazed at all the things you can see. Sometimes it's like watching a show…right outside your window! I'll bet there are some wonderful things outside your window, too!

"Looking Out My Window"

When I'm looking out my window
People come and go.
I'm just looking out my window.
Hey! There's someone that I know!
If he knew it was me watching him,
He probably would stop and say "hello."
It's really quite a show,
Looking out my window.

When I'm looking out my window,
Clouds go drifting by.
I'm just looking out my window.
There's a butterfly!
If she knew I was there she might
   fly away,
So I'm glad the butterfly doesn't know.
It's really quite a show,
Looking out my window.

I can see a tree swaying lazily.
Stretching its branches in the breeze.
And every hour another flower opens
   its petals
Just to entertain the bees.

When I'm looking out my window
Everything is new.
Looking out my window
Is my favorite thing to do.
Each and every day something's different.
There are days when you can watch the
   rain turn to snow.
It's really quite a show,
Looking out my window.
Looking out my window.
Looking out my window.

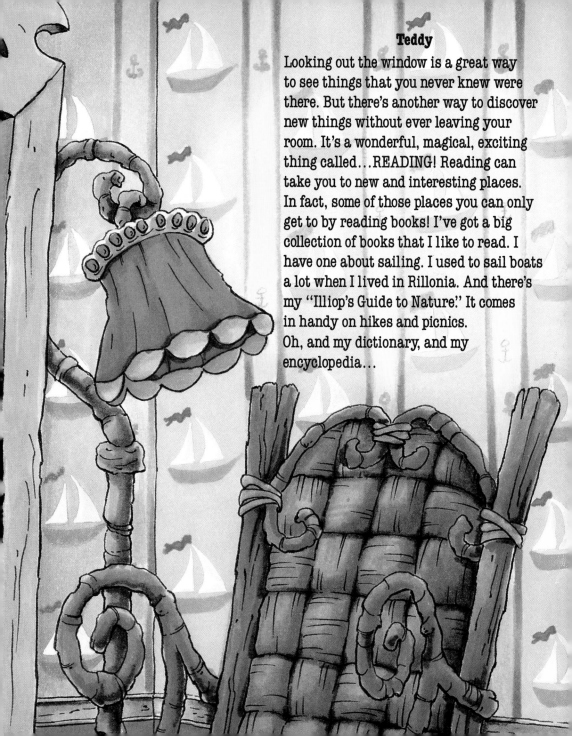

Teddy

Looking out the window is a great way to see things that you never knew were there. But there's another way to discover new things without ever leaving your room. It's a wonderful, magical, exciting thing called...READING! Reading can take you to new and interesting places. In fact, some of those places you can only get to by reading books! I've got a big collection of books that I like to read. I have one about sailing. I used to sail boats a lot when I lived in Rillonia. And there's my "Illiop's Guide to Nature." It comes in handy on hikes and picnics. Oh, and my dictionary, and my encyclopedia...

"Give A Book A Look"

I have some complicated books.
Most are really fun, though.
And one of my favorites is
"The History of Grundo"!
Oh, I also have some reference books
Which mostly you can trust in.
Hey! This old book looks interesting…
"The Story of Teddy Ruxpin."

Give a book a look, give a book a look,
  give a book a look,
Whenever the world gets dreary.
Give a book a look, give a book a look,
  give a book a look.
A good book can make you cheery,
Or take you on an adventure.
I guarantee it will be
The best trip you ever took,
If you give a book a look, give a book
  a look, give a book a look!

If there's a door you'd like to open,
A book can let you in.
There are so many books that take you
To where you've never been.
You can go to a far-off magic land
And meet a knight courageous.
When you read a book you travel just by
turning the pages!

Give a book a look, give a book a look,
give a book a look,
Whenever the world gets humdrum.
Give a book a look, give a book a look,
give a book a look,
And find out where teddy bears come from,
And you'll go on an adventure.
I guarantee it will be
The best trip you ever took,
If you give a book a look, give a book
a look, give a book a look!

Hey, here's a book about music...
"How to Play Fiddles and Flutes."
This one I just bought for Grubby...
"One Hundred Ways to Cook Roots."

Give a book a look, give a book a look,
  give a book a look,
Whenever the world gets dreary.
Give a book a look, give a book a look,
  give a book a look,
A good book can make you cheery,
Or take you on an adventure.
I guarantee it will be
The best trip you ever took,
If you give a book a look, give a book
  a look, give a book a look!
You can even come and visit me
When you give a book a look.

Teddy

So, you see, you can have fun looking out the window, or reading a book, or just imagining. Did you ever lay in bed and imagine that your blankets were something funny...or strange? If you've never tried it, just snuggle up under your covers and imagine this...

"Blankets On My Bed"

Blankets on my bed
Look like mashed potatoes.
Blankets on my bed
Aren't always what they seem.
I could pretend
They're mountains of ice cream,
And I just might eat them
When I fall asleep and dream.

Blankets on my bed,
Look just like an ocean.
Blankets on my bed,
What amazing things to see!
I imagine a starfish
Swimming up to me,
And telling me stories
All about the sea.

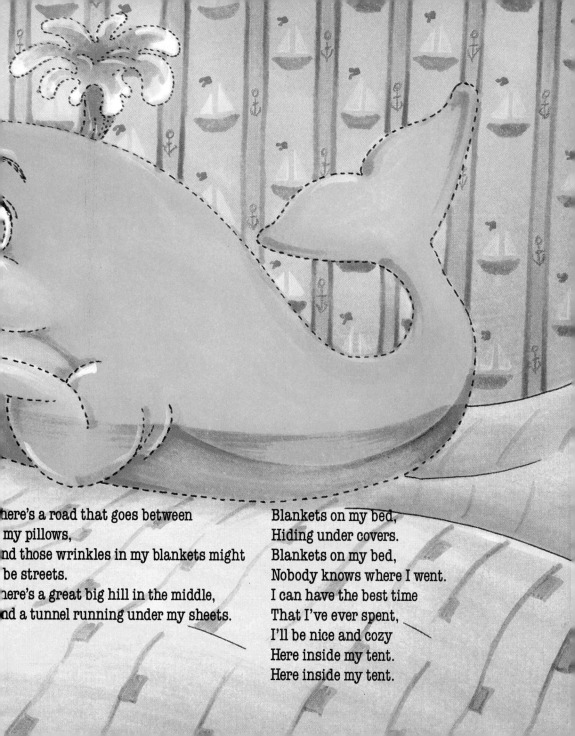

here's a road that goes between my pillows,
nd those wrinkles in my blankets might be streets.
here's a great big hill in the middle,
nd a tunnel running under my sheets.

Blankets on my bed,
Hiding under covers.
Blankets on my bed,
Nobody knows where I went.
I can have the best time
That I've ever spent,
I'll be nice and cozy
Here inside my tent.
Here inside my tent.

Teddy

Sometimes it's easier to imagine things when you're by yourself. I enjoy being alone, because I really like being with myself.

"Me, Myself and I"

I've discovered that wherever I may go,
There are always some good friends that
   I know.
I know myself, and I know I, and I know me.
And so, even when I'm all alone,
I'm in good company.

Me, myself and I,
Wherever I go, we're always together.
Me, myself and I,
We're as close as a person can be.
Oh, myself and I are always charmin' me,
And when we sing we always sing in
   three-part harmony.
I'm always happy to be,
I, myself and me!

Me, myself and I,
Wherever I go, we're always together.
Me, myself and I,
We're as close as a person can be.
Me, myself and I always try to share.
If me and myself have a party, I know
   I'll be there.
Three best friends are we,
I, myself and me!

I can do anything that I want to, when
    I'm by myself, alone.
I can stand on my head, lay in bed,
    sing a song, or write a poem.
And if I use my imagination, I can be
    anything I choose.
I can be anyplace, make a face, take
    a snooze.
I've got nothing to lose!

Me, myself and I,
Wherever I go, we're always together.
Me, myself and I,
We're as close as a person can be.
Me, myself and I, we like to chat all day.
We always know just what the others
    are gonna say.
And we always agree,
I, myself and me,
I, myself and me!

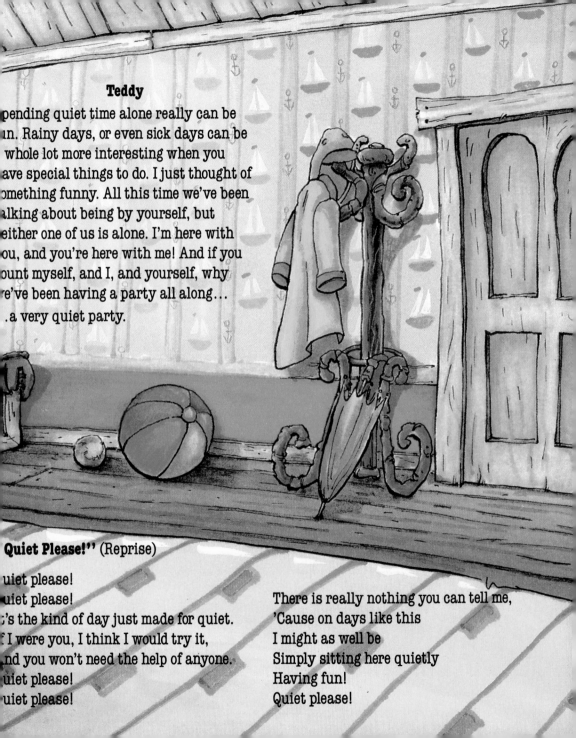

Teddy

pending quiet time alone really can be
n. Rainy days, or even sick days can be
whole lot more interesting when you
ave special things to do. I just thought of
omething funny. All this time we've been
alking about being by yourself, but
either one of us is alone. I'm here with
ou, and you're here with me! And if you
ount myself, and I, and yourself, why
e've been having a party all along...

.a very quiet party.

Quiet Please!'' (Reprise)

uiet please!
uiet please!
;'s the kind of day just made for quiet.
f I were you, I think I would try it,
nd you won't need the help of anyone.
uiet please!
uiet please!

There is really nothing you can tell me,
'Cause on days like this
I might as well be
Simply sitting here quietly
Having fun!
Quiet please!